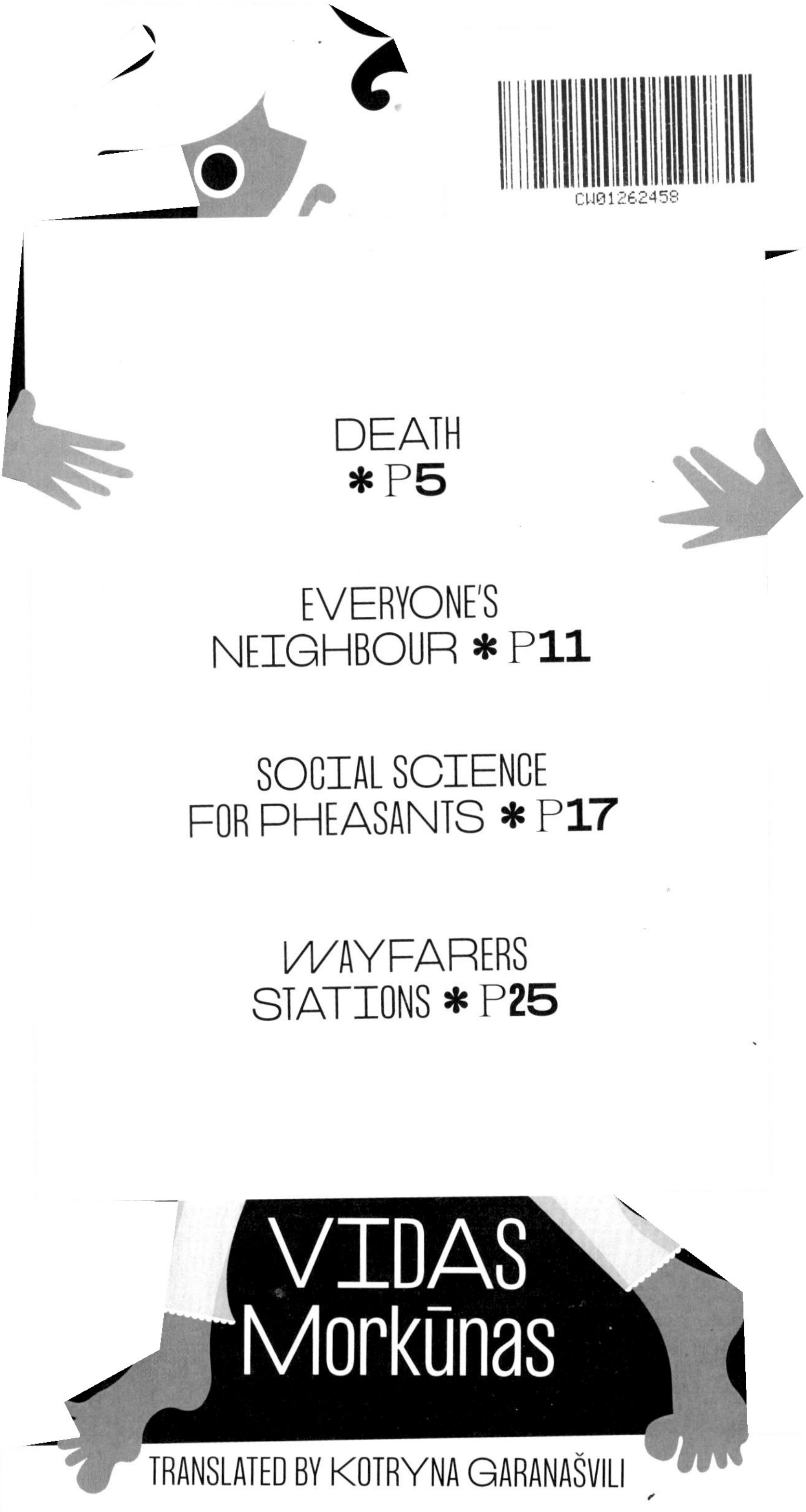

DEATH
* P**5**

EVERYONE'S
NEIGHBOUR * P**11**

SOCIAL SCIENCE
FOR PHEASANTS * P**17**

WAYFARERS
STATIONS * P**25**

VIDAS
Morkūnas

TRANSLATED BY KOTRYNA GARANAŠVILI

Death & Other Stories
Vidas Morkūnas

Translated by
Kotryna Garanašvili

First published in English by Strangers Press, Norwich, 2023
Part of UEA Publishing Project

All rights reserved
Author © Vidas Morkūnas, 2023
Translator © Kotryna Garanašvili, 2023

Printed by
Swallowtail, Norwich

Series editors
Nathan Hamilton, Aušra Kaziliūnaitė

Editorial assistance
Senica Maltese, Anita Kapočiūtė

Cover design and typesetting
Glen & Rebecca Robinson (aka GRRR.UK)

Design Copyright © 2023
Glen Robinson, Rebecca Robinson

The rights of Vidas Morkūnas to be identified as the author and Kotryna Garanašvili to be identified as the translator of this work have been asserted in accordance with the Copyright, Designs and Patents Act, 1988. This booklet is sold subject to the condition that it shall not, by way of trade or otherwise, be lent, resold, hired out, stored in a retrieval system, or otherwise circulated without the publisher's prior consent in any form of binding or cover other than that in which it is published and without a similar condition including this condition being imposed on the subsequent purchaser.

ISBN: 978-1-913861-71-1

KŪNAI was made possible by generous funding from The Lithuanian Culture Institute

Lithuanian Culture Institute

DEATH & OTHER STORIES

VIDAS Morkūnas

TRANSLATED BY KOTRYNA GARANAŠVILI

DEATH

The gravel crunched quietly under the hot rubber of my sneakers. I could already see the houses through the trees of our sparse little shaw – no mushrooms, butterflies, or animals here – when it suddenly rushed out onto the road as if chased and leapt straight into my arms. That is how I ended up taking it home.

My father promptly made a makeshift box out of plain wooden boards, attached a lid on the top, and so it came and settled with us. Or rather in a big, spacious masonry shed where our neighbours kept rabbits, hay, and all kinds of utensils, that smelled of old iron and cobwebs and in which all the neighbours kept their bicycles. The bikes that, while silent and peaceful at rest, would squeak, clack and squeal once in motion outside, each with a voice of its own. I could recognise every one.

We tried cabbage leaves, carrots, and sorrels as food, inserting them through the little hole my father left in the box for the particular purpose, but it didn't eat anything, stuck quietly there inside, probably balled up in the corner – the hole wasn't big enough for us to see through.

I intended to keep my trophy a secret, but on the very first evening, all the children crowded around and took turns pressing against the uneven, prickly boards to peek into the darkness, though they failed to discern anything. Sharp, irksome splinters pricked their palms and cheeks, and the shed gave off the strong scent of damp and potato vines as the children taunted the box, and then each other, until square dinners waited at home and their mothers were opening the windows and yelling out names.

Vidas

Eventually everyone got so used to the box they stopped noticing it. Only the neighbourhood women would bring a treat or two once in a while – a piece of homemade sausage or bacon, or perhaps some cheese – but still it refused to eat anything and eventually everyone's attention was lost.

A lone old man lived in a tiny, neat chamber up in the attic. Everyone liked him for his kindness. He never complained, never grumbled, never was nosy or sarcastic. He kept a sheep. Or rather, we knew that the animal was his, but the neighbours were happy to take care of it on account of the man's good humour; the sheep lived in the masonry, while the owner almost never left the attic and hadn't even seen his pet for quite a while. The sheep had beautiful grey wool, a black nose, and piercing, by golly, even clever eyes.

Curled up in the warm snowdrift of my bed, I listened to the raging wind; trapped in the window frame, it tossed here and there, trying to break free. An ancient draught was crawling around our enormous house, or perhaps it was already dying in some crack. It could hear the ravings of the restive younger wind too and hissed viciously: just you wait, one day you will be as knackered as me, you will be stumping over the rotting floor, sooty and pathetic, you will be whimpering in the chimney and collecting dust like a beggar, until finally you gasp your last on the threshold, crushed by the door...

During the night someone slaughtered a neighbour's rabbits – all six of them. The neighbour's first thought was of the box, so he came to see us in order to grumble. We managed to avoid a fight, but he laid the guilt on thick. We knew then that some of the neighbours were going to frown upon us from now on. We inspected the makeshift dwelling carefully – my father had lined the box with a thick layer of felt for the winter, but saw no evidence of its having escaped.

'Hey, you in there?' The owner of the unlucky rabbits kicked the box in its wooden ribs, then stood stupefied for a moment, as if stung by his own nerve. The masonry went so quiet that I thought I could almost hear the smell of rough wood and smooth stones in the walls.

And on the next morning, just before dawn a chicken, brutally maimed, almost torn in half, twitched on the frozen ground in our yard, in clear view from everyone's windows. The poor thing croaked horribly, in a voice that was no longer its own, that belonged to some other creature. It thrashed about, now trying to run, now barely crawling, but the most repulsive sight was its fierce, naïve efforts to fly. A light snow had started falling and the chicken contributed its steaming blood to the yard, but it didn't soak into the earth; the ground was covered with a thin, sparkling cloak of ice. The other chickens were scattered in little heaps, already frozen to the ground, and small puffs of the fresh, not at all wintry wind rustled their white and dark brown feathers. Those were chickens of the simplest kind. They never got any ideas – not about other chickens for instance, just like them, possibly living right next door, perhaps on the other street or even closer, right on the other side of the masonry shed. They never fooled anyone, cherished no particular ambitions, didn't crave revenge – not that they had any reason for revenge. They had nothing to fear. Do chickens – or innocent rabbits – ever wonder about perishing in a fierce battle, in a fight to the death? Without any fear, in fact with enviable calm and implicit trust, one fine morning they just look up at the hatchet in their master's hand.

    The wind kept rustling the listless feathers, one of the chickens, pressed against the masonry, raised its bloodied wing, like a flag of resistance, or surrender, its whitening eye swivelled to the sky.

    For the whole winter, the town was immersed in silence and snow, not like flour or powdered sugar, or like foam on a barber's brush – just real, unabstract snow. It crunched snugly under my warm, cumbersome winter boots; it was clean and cold, sticky enough to be rolled into perfect snowballs. It didn't cheer us much, though, because now everyone was set against us, and that meant everyone in two and a half storeys and the wings, the attic, and the extension – which was originally a barn but had long since been a dwelling – thus, all the neighbours. Some of them had neighbours of their own, living further away from us on the other side of the street, and those in turn had neighbours of their own on another street. And there were more streets in town… Moreover, the neighbours of our neighbours had relatives in other towns. Those relatives had

Vidas

neighbours, too, as well as distant relatives, whose acquaintances and folks lived in cities and, in addition to their neighbours, they had aunts, friends, and cousins abroad. What's worst: somewhere in this crowd of relatives, friends, and people you barely knew, you met occasionally, say, in the bathhouse, maybe one person – and one would be more than enough – who corresponded with a cosmonaut. Not that my father and I considered space that much.

The night frost put a lard-thick layer of rime on the window panes. I would scoop a tiny peephole in it and look at the masonry shed, wondering how it was doing in there. The yard was swamped with white, up to the windows of the ground floor. Our house seemed submerged in deep hibernation; whole days went by without a single movement or sound, except for an occasional squeak of a dreaming mouse, the quiet creak of a door hinge, a dry cough slipping into the chimney. But my father and I were shrouded in a different kind of silence, destined just for us, and its heaviness pressed on our chests, the feeling like trying to swallow a mouthful of a winter choke pear.

Despite our hardened defence, the snotty, perpetually hoarse-throated neighbourhood children still managed to attack the box, throwing snowballs in through the open door of the masonry shed. But now they didn't dare to come any closer.

I knew that during the night it crouched at the little hole in the box, its sad eye on the snowbound yard, the bright silver stars, apparently frozen on to the black velvet sky, the windows of our apartment and those of our neighbours. Was it familiar with smells and colours? Could it feel the cold? Did it wonder what the seasons were for? Did it know love? Sleep, dreams, the taste of blood?

With spring at our door, little streams murmured everywhere. I listened to the last remains of slush melting away, the winter dormancy and every grievance seeping deep into the warming ground, and the crackling, chiming sounds of life slowly waking. Tiny threads of water trickled into larger streams; the larger streams flowed along other yards and other towns into rivers, and the rivers, even further on, fell into seas I've never seen.

We decided to let it out to scurry around for a while. My father carefully removed the lid with an axe. The shadow of a pile of firewood fell over the box, making the semi-darkness inside it even darker. The interior of the box seemed larger than it could possibly be. Instinctively, we stepped backwards, turned around, and waded back home through the mud of the yard. A neighbour was watching us, or maybe the box, through the window – a kind-hearted woman who suffered from insomnia.

I was at home reading something or possibly napping, I can't remember which now, and my father was sprawled on the sofa, reading a newspaper but thinking about something else. Both of us imagined it loosening its structure, stiff after the winter: romping around, wallowing in the slushy meadow, clambering the trees, playfully chasing sparrows. It was a long and splendid day. In the evening, my father nailed the lid down again.

Spring was on a spree; the nights shrank and abated, casting quickly fading dregs of shadows on the walls and drying ground. Grass sprouted around discarded items stuck in the yard for years, along the walls and hedges; now and again, husky thunderclaps briefly shook the window panes.

In the pre-dawn twilight one morning, we were roused by the terrible bleating of the old man's sheep. In an instant, everyone in the house was bustling about. A violent thump shook our door – like someone had hit it full-force with their fist then, having vented their rage, withdrawn. The neighbours had clustered in the corridors and kitchens, waiting. Children crowded under the stairs. One could almost believe that the worn treads of the stairs themselves were whispering and giggling. No one dared step outside. In the yard near the door, the sheep thrashed, bleating like crazy. Dawn was already upon us. Nothing had happened to the animal. But its owner, the old man who lived upstairs, had died.

Unnoticed by anyone, I sneaked up to the attic. An alarm clock ticked away on a nightstand, as if nothing had happened. A small, cast-iron stove was wasting heat. The deceased lay under the warm bedspread, his head tilted slightly to one side. He watched me out of the corner of his glassy eye. He looked just as he always did. His sallow face was not drawn into an ugly grimace; when he was alive, his features were not hideous. It didn't seem like the

Vidas

old body had been tormented by any convulsions, his soul was not weighed down with woeful sins. A draught crept into the room and dissipated the stale air a little, then began to play with a strand of his grey hair. I could see the sliver of a great white cloud through the window. Hollow bleats from the by now exhausted sheep still welled up from the yard. The animal wasn't aware that its master had experienced no horror or pain, that he'd simply gone to bed and departed.

The neighbours were unyielding. They refused any contribution to the funeral from my father and me, didn't even allow us to come anywhere near the ceremony. Any communication between us and the neighbours ceased entirely. Still, we were lucky enough not to be exiled to some other town. We found the box with a hole axed in the lid and some obvious traces of a strong chemical. It was gone.

I tried to look for it throughout the summer, until late autumn brought the frost. Once I heard people saying that it was seen settled on the slippery stones in our brook, scooping bleaks. I raced there but all I saw were the pale bellies of some little fish in the stream. This was the last we heard of it. It wasn't like I could just place an announcement in the newspaper: Missing...

Albeit slowly, our neighbours' attitudes towards us did thaw. We are now on a warm and sincere footing again. The fowl gabble endlessly in the yard, the masonry shed smells of dry firewood and pickled cabbage. The days are shrinking and receding once more, leaving slivers of clear light on the walls, roofs, and clouds. All would be well if not for a lingering resentment that now I'll never know what it looked like.

EVERYONE'S NEIGHBOUR

The moon spreads a tin-cold rug next to her bed, just as it has done every night for the past thirty years. Dust gathered on a lone shelf, on the cupboard, on the lampshade also, the same as always. The girl wipes it away but slowly it settles down again. In this house, even the annual begonia has remained the same for thirty years. Old, withered, having suffered all possible floral diseases, it blooms shorter each year, and more humbly, but still it sucks all it can from the sooty soil in its yellow flowerpot. Only the innumerable generations of flies have changed over the course of three decades.

Dresses hang in the wardrobe, the door of which creaks terribly whenever it is opened. They should have been worn to shreds, yet they survive, sensing somehow their presence is needed and valued. Small glasses clink in the china cupboard whenever the draught makes its way in. They have never tasted any liquid, except an occasional stream of water to wash their closed little throats. In this house, the radio that transmits a single station and the old alarm clock that has buzzed at exactly the same hour and minute every day for the past thirty years, are thick as thieves. The moment the two of them start to chatter, one after the other, the mistress of the house gets out of bed and pulls on her slippers, and so her day begins.

Before setting out, the girl is wrapped cosily by her coat. It is uniquely cut but prone to catching cold. Relations between its elements have become strained. The back, the chest, the sleeves, the tails, and the pockets have been far from friendly for a while now; some parts are no longer even properly acquainted, but patiently they keep together out of a sense of duty approaching habit, for nothing else will warm their mistress through the raw autumn and leaden winter, nothing else will cover her stooping shoulders. A pair of boots moans and complains as it slips over her feet – its leather wrinkled and beaten beyond the repair of polish. A balding brush offers the only consolation.

Vidas

Crunching under her feet, the snow doesn't stay fresh for long, it melts mixing with salt and mud crumbled from a great many pairs of shoes. The snow remains clean in the still air, but wilts with the fatigue of the elderly coats, the scruffy furs, and the weary heads it touches, with some of their sickness and anger. The whiteness lingers only in the woods and impracticable fields, places far removed from the chimney soot and the cars, the people and the dogs. In spring the secrets snow has kept are revealed: empty, now pungent milk cartons, fossilised crusts of bread, crumpled cigarette packs, used sanitary pads, a miserable spruce skeleton here, dismal bicycle bones there. Everything stays so until the next autumn, the next winter. Maybe something will be pilfered by children or picked up by the caretaker, but then the wind will step in, racing into the overflowing dumpsters, blowing over the dumping grounds, depositing back something like an old fishbone, a curdy condom, a shred of a map, the stub of a cigarette the smoker of which might as well be rotting too, six feet under – then the snow will cover everything once again.

Crunching under her feet, the snow doesn't have the slightest impact on her feelings. She makes her way up the slippery stairs and tears open the door, behind which she'll spend the whole day. Here's her old chair – slightly rickety, but still fairly firm, much like the desk. She has lived for a long time by their side, without either intense sentiment or conflict. She takes a seat, and a stream of letters and parcels begin to flow through her fingers. Once upon a time, cosmonauts and scientists, secretaries and nameless athletes, used to smile at her. Once upon a time, she accidentally learned the Latin names of flowers and animals and got acquainted, in passing, with classic painting. But on her way to work or back home, she has never met a single Latin person to whom she could say *Vulpes vulpes* or *Lutra lutra*. No more cosmonauts now. Only birds, wayside shrines and national costumes, nothing more.

She always spends her lunch break – not one second over an hour – in the diner in the basement of the same building. Yellowed curtains barely cover the shoes of the many passers-by moving behind the small windows. Chairs made of wood and aluminium stab the wrinkled linoleum; in places, it has become so loose and tattered that it makes the tables quiver, opening cold patches of concrete that collect glistening sugar crystals, old crumbs of a pie removed from the menu ages ago, obsolete coins. Her diet hasn't changed for years. The plump waitress behind the counter knows it by heart: whitewashed curd, glue soup, rubber schnitzel, a cup of geodesic coffee, and a piece of counterfeit cake. The smell of stale mayonnaise gathers like mist under the ceiling, and the scent of cheap wine flutters in a faint draught close to the floor. When the two of them blend above the tabletops, the diner will have to be shut down for a while. But for now... An aluminium spoon dives into the coffee, as she wearily drowns the sugar; the persistent feet behind the half-windows trample the already mushy snow. The pigeons defecate in the attic.

In the evening, she pushes through the door into the weighty dusk and heads back home. Her slouched shoulders, her threadbare coat, her old-fashioned bun, old-fashioned glasses: what would become of this town if these things were torn from her exterior? She never looks down to the ground or up to the sky, or around; her surroundings haven't changed in decades.

The cold walls of the stairwell are painted deep green and covered in writing like a diary or a register of other people's secrets. The musty odour of urine – human, rat, or both – lingers inside, despite the constant draughts. Home, at last. Squeaky floor and an amber mosaic of a landscape on the wall. A handful of books on a half-empty shelf: *Mushroom Recipes, The Alchemist, Alice in Wonderland, Pastries*... A single grey hair on the shabby doormat, the smell of onions in the tiny kitchen.

Summer is the time for a vacation. She doesn't go anywhere but spends her days knitting and cleaning the dust. Children and dogs yammer in the backyard. Neighbours quarrel behind the wall. The shadows of trees breach through the windows, the smell of stewed cabbage wafts from the neighbouring kitchens. Ah, summer.

She went to a resort once. The sea was dark grey, almost blue, the sand light yellow. She was disappointed. Those were not the colours she'd hoped for. Worse, in the swarm of people most were naked. She went to a diner at the foot of the sand dunes, close to the public toilets, where the smell of chebureki was so intense

Vidas

you could almost sink your teeth into it. She was pestered by an intrusive man, most probably a pervert: Are you all right? Can I help you? She was annoyed by the overly polite waitress, the slamming doors, and the linoleum scrubbed to the quick. A particularly fat man at the next table was whistling, panting, creaking, and hissing, and talking to everyone around him in the interim. She left without finishing her meal. Another man stood at the corner of the diner, propped with one hand against the tin-panelled wall and vomiting painfully. When he looked up, she flinched. She could have sworn it was the cosmonaut she had secretly and hopelessly loved seventeen years ago. But that man, the one on a stamp, had on a spacesuit and a happy smile gleaming from within his helmet. This one, to be sure, had neither. His puffy, purple face looked like it hadn't smiled for seventeen years, at least.

Even before the holiday ended, she was only too eager to leave the resort where no one was embarrassed by their bulging bellies, bloated underbellies and saggy breasts, where the pine trees smelled bizarrely of some medicament, and returned home – albeit with a splinter in her heart. Her only consolation was the thought of the money she had managed to save by not buying a swimsuit.

She walked from the station with her shoulders hunched, impatient to get home. In the front yard, she looked up at the windows of her apartment and a shiver of cold, horror and longing had run through her body – her kitchen window was glowing in the twilight. As she made her way slowly up the crumbling stairs, her legs trembled. The whole staircase reeked of urine and mould. I must be seeing things, she thought as she turned the key with shaking hands. The fish in the bowl had missed her badly, one of them was already dead. It smelled of wallpaper and stale bread. The neighbours were quarrelling behind the wall. She felt wrapped in peace and warmth. She had just forgotten to turn off the light in the kitchen. The loyal 60W bulb had waited patiently for her to return, only to then explode, stricken by a heart attack.

With summer gone, autumn starts to seep slowly into human bodies, buildings, public transport, dogs, cats, sparrows, even pigeons. Only crows retain their independence from the seasons. They shake the last leaves from the trees with their sharp voices, drag stolen chunks of meat along the pavements, and argue constantly with one another.

The girl takes the coat from her wardrobe. It looks even more tattered, not rested at all throughout summer. Almost transparent now, with fraying sleeves. She holds her devoted friend up to the light to inspect it, then starts the surgery. The coat squeaks with pain and sighs with gratitude before it finally calms down, hung in the hallway.

And again, every day, from early morning to late afternoon , she moves the parcels, sticks the post stamps, hands out registered letters. At lunch, another waitress serves her a cup of the same coffee. The head of the department, as before, sneezes and blows his nose at the next table. On the other side of the window – cracked now, which is a change, at least – the same feet tread along the same pavement, the same words are muttered, the same smell of mayonnaise hangs, the coffee maker spews the same steam, like yesterday, the day before yesterday, ten years ago. Suddenly she's filled with an urge to regurgitate the despair sitting deep inside her, like a chestnut stuck in her throat, and spit it out – to scream at the damned mayonnaise that it stinks, to tell the shoes on the other side of the windows that they are dirty and long out of fashion, to scold the head of the department how rude is to snivel where other people eat. Instead, she chokes on her cold coffee and runs out embarrassed.

In the evening the girl, as usual, makes herself a cup of tea, spreads some butter on a slice of bread, reads the gardener's companion, brushes her teeth, washes and dries her face, looks in the mirror, closes her eyes, opens them again, combs her hair, and starts to undress. She puts on a nightgown. It smells of the plywood of the bedding chest. She winds the alarm clock. Suddenly, surprisingly, the doorbell buzzes and she is stupefied. Expectation of some surprise, fear and longing turn her joints into ice, render her almost insensible. Not for long though. A moment later she creeps to the door and peeks gingerly through the peephole. There's no one in the stairwell. She stifles a sigh and goes back into the room. And can't remember if she wound the alarm clock.

Vidas

That night, tired of sleeplessness, she gets up from bed and sets the alarm – again. This unbearable workload (in addition to old age) causes the device to finally expire and when the time comes to announce the new morning, the clock is already dying and cannot fully buzz. One last weak tick is followed by deathly silence. Sound asleep, the girl is unaware of the tragedy and for the first time in her life is late for work. In the bright November late-morning, her face is whipped by a fiery hailstorm of passing gazes. She slogs by, her shoulders more hunched than ever, the massive door even more reluctant as she gives it a push on arrival. To top it all, she finds a bowl of flowers on her desk – oh, why oh why such cruel jeers? The remaining hours pass by in suffering. She avoids going anywhere for lunch. By the end of the afternoon, she realises she no longer knows anything – dates, names, and routes, it all escape her. Only late in the evening she finally makes her way home, dishevelled, her sides dirty, dazed. She unbuttons her coat with frozen fingers, pulls off her boots, throws them to the corner of the room and tumbles into her bed without even turning on the light.

At three in the morning, a grey lump flattens itself against the fish bowl. It slides down the glass, scaring the fish, then shoots up and melts into the ceiling.

Seven seconds past half past seven, a switch turns untouched and fills the room with light. In the kitchen, fire starts under the kettle, and soon, the water is boiling. The fridge door and the breadbin open, a smooth layer of butter spreads on a slice of bread. At the same time in the anteroom, the balding brush zealously polishes the boots, while the black coat rubs yesterday's dirt from its sides with its sleeves. A switch shifts its position again. She remains lying in the dark, her eyes and mouth slightly open. The door unlocks and obligingly lets the coat and the shoes wander out, then closes again. They saunter down the stairs familiar since childhood, plod along the familiar path. The caretaker recognises the passing silhouette, greets it with a good morning, and shrugs his shoulders, as he unexpectedly receives no response.

SOCIAL SCIENCE FOR PHEASANTS

'If you know where to point your spyglass, you'll always find something. There's a man from the neighbouring five-storey apartment building, convinced no one can see him, taking his trash up on the roof. I see him, though. I see the shameless couples, too, making out behind shabby grey kiosks. I live on the seventh floor, I see everything. The men loitering at the shop and the bottle depot where my friend works. The everlasting old women of the little market. The huge Y-shaped footpath that runs across the bare field, its main part leading off towards the 'centre' – that is, the depot, the kiosks, the shop and the little market, – while the two branches lead towards our own seven-storey apartment building and the five-storey building opposite. Nothing but wasteland all around. Only a highway further on, linked to the 'centre' by the narrow, bumpy road.

Vidas

The sounds are quieter during the day, but the echoing howl of the elevator is clear at night. Just like the clack of the garbage chute door. Just like the drunken quarrels of the neighbours. In the evenings, spotted teenagers with sagging pants settle down on the small benches under the awning by the entrance. Guitars have gone out of fashion.

The stairwell on the first floor, specked with cigarette marks and scribble, gives off the sour smell of damp and cabbage soup. I don't know the lives of the people in the neighbouring building, but in our house time goes by slowly and monotonously. If the more distant neighbours pass away or move somewhere else, we often don't notice.

Next day I was going to visit my son at the boarding school. I had to set off on a rather long journey early in the morning, so I made preparations in the evening: bought a couple kilograms of barley in the shop and half a bucket of raspberries in the little market. My friend from the depot was going to take the weeks' worth of empty bottles to the seaport glass factory. Same way I needed to go, so I enjoyed the chance to grab a ride.

For quite a while in my free time I've been crafting this walker – as a present for my son, who was returning for holiday in a month's time. Now I worked on it for a bit, then placed it in the corner of the hall and swept up the remains: pieces of paper smeared with glue, twisted nails, offcuts of wood. I was going to take out the trash first, then collect my tools, but as soon as I opened the door, a little beast jumped inside, slipped between my legs and ended up at the door of my son's room. I couldn't really see at first what kind of creature it was. When it started scratching the bottom of the door, it annoyed me. I forgot the trash bag and had the whole set of tools around me from which to choose a weapon. I eyed the intruder. The body was long and lean, the animal seemed sickly, its left ear torn and bleeding, and its brown-and-grey fur shabby, dishevelled. A rabid one! I thought. Meanwhile, the beast scraped, persistently, at the corner of my son's door. I considered various ways to get it out of there without touching it – I didn't want to get scratched, or, even worse, bitten. At first, I grabbed a broomstick and poked the beast on the nape of the neck with the long handle. It made a sound between a growl and a squeak, but didn't look at me. This impudence made my blood boil. I poked with the broomstick again, this time aiming at its side, but missed. I was hoping to press the brute to the door and, changing my own position, push it slowly out into the stairwell, but the beast turned to face me and, sitting down on the floor, observed me intently for a few seconds. Its gaze made me even more furious. I stabbed at it again and this time hit its eye. The beast screeched horribly. Fidgeting all over the place, stupefied with pain, it jumped on the door handle and slipped, then smashed heavily onto the floor. That couple of seconds was enough for me to grab another weapon, a hammer. Yelping and splashing around drops of blood, the beast spun around itself. I didn't wait for it to recover and smacked it on its back with the broomstick with all my rage, as far as the cramped space would allow, again and again. Poor thing tried to escape my thumps but it was awkward, probably too weakened by now. Just squirmed and whined pathetically. Still it managed to jump onto the unfinished walker. And then I lost it. With the first strike of the hammer, I hit the beast's leg, almost tearing it off, leaving it hanging by a flap of skin. The second strike smashed its skull. Blinded with rage, I brought down the third and the fourth strikes on the walker, smashing all my hard work to pieces. At last coming back to my senses I dropped the hammer. Not much was left of the beast. I picked up the bloody remains with pliers like a dirty rag, brought it out to the stairwell and threw it into the garbage shaft. Pressing my ear to the pipe covered from top to bottom in crumbling yellow paint, I listened for a few moments to the sound of the pitiful little body sliding down. It took me a while to get everything and myself cleaned. Then I went to my son's room and found among his books a copy of *Animals of the World* by Tadas Ivanauskas. After leafing through illustrations and doing a bit of reading, I found out that the intruder must have been a stone marten. How it ended up in our wasteland, and on the seventh floor of the apartment building at that, I didn't even imagine then.

    Early next morning, my friend and I took to the road in a wildly thrumming truck, clinking with empties as we drove towards the seaport. My friend was talking a mile a minute, which was

Vidas

fine by me. Lately he'd been investigating a juicy idea – whether, if drinking from the neck of the bottle, one may leave their soul inside. My friend was already deep into considerations on the matter and generously shared his thoughts. My own kept returning to the previous night's incident with the marten, so I had no wish to ask what happens if, for example, the same person repeatedly drinks from the necks of various bottles. I was quiet and just nodded my head. Nevertheless, his talk about the glass factory, the scariest place in the world, as he called it, did grip my attention. 'Can you imagine how many souls must be trapped in there?'

The long journey didn't feel very long, but, when my friend stopped to let me out at the exit to the small country lane leading to the boarding school, I still sighed with relief.

I had left a couple of kilometres still to go but it was nothing but a pleasure walking on a beautiful forenoon in early autumn such as this. I treaded the lane, a brisk wind ruffling my hair, rustling the tall roadside grass. My spirits were high. The route ahead slipped between two birch trees, then climbed up a low hill. I stopped at the top and could see the grounds stretching below. I shivered with excitement. Located in a former Pioneer camp, the boarding school was wallowing in a summerly greenery, the colourful roofs of the buildings poking out like mushroom caps. Several ponds glistened on the left side. I couldn't make out the building of the fur-feathers-scales recycling factory – its low chimneys were obscured by the trees.

A polite employee let me in through the gate and I peeked inside the closest cottage. A couple were seated behind a plain wooden table. The middle-aged man stared at the floor with his head bowed, holding it in both hands. The woman, of a similar age, probably his wife, was wiping away tears, sniffling. A little cage was placed on the table. Inside, a small orange bird hopped monotonously, even indifferently, from one perch to the next.

I knew I had to pass the classrooms of mice, lizards, and foxes, then turn right just before the pond. Walking the light-brown, gravelled footpath, with immaculately cut lawns on both sides, I followed the directions carefully. Here was mine: PHEASANTS.

A new, increasingly popular trend of the pedagogy of integration suggested placing the children moulded into foxes next to the children moulded into pheasants. The reason being that, in many cases, children who ended up in the foxes class exceeded approved limits in naivety and sincerity, calculated by a complex formula, while children who had an overly high rate of shyness and humility became pheasants. Based on the idea that the two species might be better integrated, education programmes were prepared trying to find things that foxes and pheasants had in common. On the other side, the pheasants were paired with the earthworms, the parents of the latter wanting their children to get to know the smell and taste of the black earth, instead of having their heads so up in the clouds. Following the security requirements, it was strictly forbidden to bring any presents containing animal products.

The education programmes of some other classes seemed rather odd to me. For instance, mice children were taught to be nosy and determined, while the amoebas were to focus on modesty. I visited the meeting room of the latter class once out of sheer curiosity – leaning over the microscopes, the visiting parents looked like scientists of some sort. The concept of educating the bees was even stranger – these children were being prepared for social work, and were paired with hedgehogs.

The transformer house – the location of the department for transforming a human into an animal and back again – was located at the very edge of the vast grounds with a separate driveway. Any contact between the former students of the boarding school – those who graduated successfully and those who failed – with the current intake was strictly prohibited. For some reason, the prohibition also applied to alumni who decided to remain in their animal form after graduation.

The buildings of the pheasant class edged into an assembly of aviaries of different sizes. Approaching, I found them empty. Perhaps the studies were taking place inside. As soon as I entered the two-storey building, painted in vivid colours to match the colouring of the students, the deputy principal appeared before me, a petite, humble-looking woman, her face darkened with fatigue.

'Respected parent, respected parent,' she chirped, all prim and proper. 'Please, do come in, it is our pleasure to have you here.'

Vidas

The walls of the long corridor were covered in photographs depicting the life of the boarding house, the celebrations, the portraits of high achievers – pheasants, quails, partridges and some other birds, I didn't recognize them all. Plaques, souvenirs, and prizes won by the boarding house and its students were placed in a glass cupboard. I could hear muffled chirping, screeching cackling behind the classroom doors.

'The pheasants are in a social studies lesson right now, while the peacocks have ethics,' explained the deputy principal.

We went into her office and sat down on a sofa at a small coffee table. She offered me some barley coffee and oat biscuits. We exchanged a couple of remarks about my journey here and the weather. The deputy principal, who kept glancing anxiously at the things I brought with me – the barley and the raspberries – finally seemed to brace herself and poured forth the news. I was astonished to discover that my son was no longer a member of the pheasant class, that the psychological pressure had become too hard for him in that group, and that the educational board, after careful considerations with the experts, of course, decided to move him to the marten class.

'But... I only wanted him to pick up a bit of flying,' I stuttered, probably blanching like a ghost. 'Spiritually, at least.'

The schoolteacher spluttered her apologies, tried to convince me that the boarding school would accept full responsibility for not informing me of the changes, and eventually declared that the direct transformation from one animal into another, skipping the human state, while unique, was not at all dangerous. She even offered to take me to the marten class. Bowing like a fool, I said I would find the way by myself, grabbed the goods I'd brought with me and hurried to bid farewell. The teacher seemed relieved. As I stumbled out into the corridor, a beautiful pheasant was striding by wagging its head. The pearly sheen of its vivid colours. Before realizing it, I took a handful of barley and scattered it on the parquet floor. The bird looked at me in amazement.

Dazed, I blundered around the boarding school until I found the marten class. The cages in which the cute little grey-and-brown creatures lived were aligned in a long row. Recovering a little,

Morkūnas

I walked slowly past their wire houses. Most of the martens were pattering restlessly in their boxes, some were jumping lively up and down the walls, a few were simply lying indifferently on the floor.

'Respected parent, our respected parent,' I heard the same words, in a shrill voice this time. 'Please come in, the pleasure is ours'

I had almost reached an empty cage, but another woman – the supervisor of my son's class, as I soon found out – took my arm in a persistently polite way, and dragged me away. We entered a two-storey building painted in grey and brown. Here again the walls of the long corridor were covered in photographs: the life of the boarding house, the high achievers – martens, sables, otters. Prizes and souvenirs in a glass cupboard. The teacher took me to her office, but no coffee or biscuits were offered. She invited me to sit down and then left. In a short while, she returned, quite perplexed, and asked me if I could wait for my son in the meeting cottage. I spared her any explanations. Just nodded vacantly and left.

The meeting cottages of the boarding school were furnished moderately. A table, wooden benches, modest curtains on the window. No grandeur, no decoration. A vase of flowers, at most.

I sat with my head bent, holding it in both hands, staring at the floor. Waiting for something, but what? Perhaps there still was a spark of hope somewhere in the depths of my subconscious.

Finally, a steward brought in a marten in a rather large cage. It was a very beautiful beast. Smooth, shiny light brown fur and a glaringly white collar. For a minute or two, the marten buzzed nervously around the cage. Then it suddenly stiffened and pierced me with the penetrating gaze of its beady black eyes.

'You are not my son!' I hissed, barely containing my rage.

The animal sat down, bent its back, and started scratching its ear with its claws.

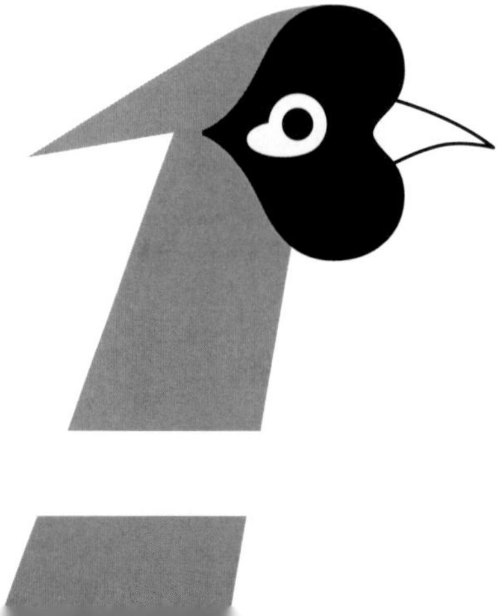

WAYFARERS STATIONS

***/stations

My friend offered to show me a fresco, a unique one according to him, visible on the masonry wall of a derelict church, only for a short while, when the rays of the evening sun touched it at the necessary angle. We reached the inner yard of the monastery by a narrow path that instantly disappeared into the deep greenery of tall grass shrouded by lumps of fallen bricks and various dumped utensils of unknown age and origin.

We had to watch our step; glass shards were hidden along our path. At the far side of the yard, a huge pit gaped, filled with saplings and shrubs, and a load of junk had been piled up on its edge: a door peppered with holes, old armchairs reaching out with their springs, tattered shoes, plaster spalls. I lingered at the junk pile to photograph the stray shoes for a colleague, a collector of such pictures. When I returned, my friend was sitting on a pile of three bricks under some ancient, gnarled apple trees. The bark on the twisted trunks was peeling off in big patches, apparently ready to crumble once touched. Drifters had made camp under the apple trees: the black remains of a small fire with two protruding spikes, an old ragged coat tossed nearby. My friend thumbed the pages of a book he'd found, giggling.

'Imagine that,' he said. 'It tells the story of two guys travelling to an abandoned monastery to see a fresco!'

Vidas

I leaned forward to take a look. I couldn't see the author's name, only the title, *Wayfarers Stations*. I didn't know the book. He put it back where he'd found it and stood up, then waded towards the church, stepping high, sweeping the grass with the flaps of his black raincoat. I followed his lead. A bat flitted over my head, drawing lopsided figures in the air, almost too fast to notice.

We clambered over the remains of a demolished wall and found ourselves in a former temple. It was drearily silent, only the clumps of stonework and plaster made crackling sounds under our feet. The few dusty pews that remained were reminiscent to my friend of dismantled pianos and to me of classroom desks. Shreds of coloured glass glistened on the floor, scattered here and there under the gaping holes of the arched little windows. My friend instinctively removed his fancy hat as we tilted our heads to look up at the space between two empty apertures. The wall resembled a map of a world, one unknown to us. We waited patiently, still, silent for some time. Finally, a narrow strip of evening light illuminated the rugged, crumbling plaster and started to widen...

Morkūnas

***/the bottomless

ᶜThey met by accident at the station. They hadn't seen each other for years, but recognised each other at once. Alfukas had a skill for asking favours in a way no one could refuse, and so Remigijus agreed to drive him home.

The ride was only two and a half kilometres long. At first, it looked like they'd have something to talk about. But Remigijus soon fell silent.

'...knockedoffa...fuckingdick...whatevernotlikeIgiveafuck.' Alfukas was sputtering some sort of gibberish.

A sense of excitement burned in Remigijus's chest. He had never been in the company of a serious criminal before. I wonder how many people he's killed, he thought, while feeling simultaneously ashamed at his own curiosity.

As they drove out of the little town, Alfukas, too, fell silent. He was looking indifferently through the window at the autumnal gardens and bare windswept shrubs rushing past. Remigijus stole a glance at his companion's scarred, prematurely creased face.

How strange, he thought. If I returned home after so many years, I wouldn't ask for a ride. I'd walk, want to absorb everything, greedy for the air of my childhood fields...

They turned into a narrow path overgrown with thick shrubs, almost invisible now, and soon reached the returnee's house on the edge of the forest. It was a ramshackle wreck. Alfukas got out, while Remigijus remained politely in the car.

He probably needs some privacy, he thought. I'd better not get in the way.

His companion had left a faint stink in the car – not a fart, nor cheap vodka – something much darker, heavier.

His irritation growing by the minute, Alfukas waded into the tall, yellowed grass, then stepped inside, trod on glass shards and cinder, then kicked at the various now mouldy pieces of junk. On his way home, he'd expected to find people and, surely, at least something valuable in their possession. But the house had been deserted a long time and anything missed by the thieves had been burned, or broken, or had rotted, rusted.

Vidas

I should get rid of that moron, he thought. That wreck of his won't get me far, though. I'd fuck it up at the nearest turn. Let him take me somewhere else, and then I'll sort it.

Alfukas returned to the car with a pair of gumboots in his hand. They were covered in a thick layer of something, probably manure from a decrepit cowshed nearby – their insides were stuck together, so you could hardly insert your foot.

'Want them? Fiver.' Asked Alfukas when they were back on the highway. He was still holding the boots in his arms for some reason.

'Why would I want them?' replied Remigijus with a shy smile.

'Well, I don't fucking need them,' said Alfukas, dully. He opened the window and threw them out.

One of the boots flew straight into the shallow water of a ditch, the other bumped and rolled and finally slumped down in the middle of the road and remained there.

Morkūnas

*** /the nameless

When I first saw him, after forty-six years, it was his eyes that helped me recognise him, that same light but piercing blue gaze. The child of the past, as I found out, had spent almost his whole life in a tuberculosis ward, and now was a splay-legged, hunched and sickly older man in faded charity garments. His thin, greying hair, swept over the top of his head, hardly covered the bald dome spattered with pink spots. Like all those years back we stood by the tall pedestal with the large stone pot, like a salad-bowl, on top of it.

In front of the façade of a former manor, there was a plain wire construction enlaced by bare ivy growths with an opening big enough to walk through. In the summer, this mesh of greenery would turn into a pretty hedgerow, but back then, forty-six years ago, there had been no hedgerow. Everything else, however, looked almost the same. The same buildings, pale yellow and grey, as if deliberately painted to match the hue of the patients' skin, the same ruins in the park and the same crows croaking in the trees, which had grown considerably; the same ancient stone chalices with flowers sprouting from them – the crumbling pedestal of one of which had recently been patched up with some bricks. Even the air surrounding the sanatorium seemed unchanged in nearly five decades; just as before, it was steeped in molecules of infection and sadness, saturated with premonitions of the end. Suddenly, I felt afraid to see the *latvija* minibus again, its windowless cabin, parked next to the gaunt building, more squat than all the others on the right hand side. For a moment I envisioned the empty, reverberant corridors of the main block, the uninviting spaces smelling of medication, redolent with loneliness.

My childhood playmate of half-a-day told me the story of his life, pausing now and again, smiling shyly. For many years, he came here for treatment and, eventually, left on his own, lonely and forgotten by his relatives and scant acquaintances, he settled into the sanatorium for good. When things changed and it was transformed into a modern mental institution, my companion was kindly provided with an appropriate diagnosis and this is

Vidas

how he had remained in the pale yellow mansion – along with the numerous others brought here from hospitals, prisons, and various 'loony-bins'.

    Back then, forty-six years ago, I hadn't memorised the boy's name. Now, I didn't ask.

Morkūnas

*** /encaustic

They pulled back the edge of the carpet. Edmutis didn't deserve any comfort. The whiff of old dust filled the living room. The exposed floor was light brown.

He kneeled in the doorway as he was told and crawled, almost perkily, across the room, right up to his granny, who was seated in the corner. He paused in front of her, afraid to touch the old woman's knees, then bent over, per his instructions, and kissed her dry, yellowed, veined hand. It looks like that tree branch in the museum, in the nature section, thought the child, feeling a bit embarrassed by the comparison. A sour smell hit his nostrils. Following further instructions, he returned to the doorway, still on his knees, then crawled back to his granny to kiss her hand again. Not as perkily this time. On the fifth crawl, he twisted his patella and felt a sudden jolt of pain in his already aching knee. The boy did his best to keep his composure but on the eighth crawl he could no longer contain himself, and a treacherous tear splashed onto the floor. His folks stood in the antechamber, talking. Every once in a while one of them would remind Edmutis of the number. Approaching his granny again, he glanced through the window at the clouds drifting across the sky and tried to imagine what was going on in the park, where they had carousels, airplanes and a Ferris wheel, ice cream and lemonade. He felt a painful pinch on his heart.

Slogging along for the seventeenth time, Edmutis was smiling. Despite his sore knees, back, and neck, despite the suspicious glances from his folks. Though there might be a cost to pay for the smile, the child wasn't sure himself at what point his hatred had disappeared, at what point he'd lost determination to love everyone better than before, at what point his lust for vengeance had dissipated. When he crawled over for the nineteenth time, his granny suddenly withdrew her hand. She was already bored by the punishment.

Vidas

***/the wealthy

On the day their love was kindled in the small canteen at their school, borscht, schnitzel, and compote were served for dinner. Same old, more or less. As always, the children bustled around; the gym teacher with the surname of a bird made jokes while eating; the faded, worn linoleum squeaked underneath the chairs; the dishes rattled. Raising a fork to her mouth, she raised her eyes too and peeked at the swarthy young man with curly hair and thick glasses who sat opposite her, just a quick glance, but it determined much of their lives thereafter. He felt the glance but didn't let it show, just hunched his shoulders even more, felt confused, and leaned over the already half-empty plate of pink liquid to brush some invisible breadcrumbs from the top of the table. Then he stole a glance at her himself, and was filled with an incredible warmth – no formula could express it. Both of them were mathematicians, both short-sighted, but the rims of her glasses were of thin metal wire, while the rims of his glasses were bulky, and made of antler bone.

    They arrived for dinner together and, together, left the little canteen. And they stayed together. They checked over pupils' homework, summoned the parents of the mischievous and lazy kids, went to professional training sessions and sometimes sightseeing tours, always together. They moved to another school, also together. Wherever they went, whatever they did, they were always together, cuddling, holding hands. The students would giggle, the colleagues would scoff behind their backs, but they didn't care. They were inseparable. Many years later even, when they both went blind, it happened at almost the same time, but she lost her sight just a little before.

Morkūnas

***/the early

Anetė wasn't coming to our house anymore. I knew the reason she was aggrieved. She was six months older than me but there was a simple word she still couldn't pronounce correctly: *candy*. She would say *gandy*. *Gandy, gandy, gandy*. All my efforts to teach her otherwise were in vain. Having lost my last bit of patience, I had scoffed at her. I had two candies. So I showed them to her purposefully. But I didn't give her any. Alas, I said, what a pity, I have no *gandies*, I would give them to you if I had. She stood there biting her lip, without saying a word. I could see she was beyond herself with the itch for a candy. Still I didn't give her any. I was trying to nurture my patience. I would have gladly given her all the candies in the world, but I couldn't betray myself. If I declared my love first, what kind of a man would that make of me? Anetė snuffled her nose, the most beautiful nose in the neighbourhood, and brushed it with the back of her hand, which she then rubbed softly against the front of her mottled fur coat – as if it were the real fur of some animal. A glistening streak clung to her chest. With her head down, she shuffled by our neighbours' sheds towards her home. I almost followed her like a puppy. I could never get enough of watching that shuffling gait. But I deliberately turned around and ran. I was trying to nurture my patience, after all.

Eventually, I could endure it no longer. So from all sorts of hiding places, I collected the candies – all right, all right, *gandies* – I'd been stashing away patiently for a long time – some already suspiciously hardened – and, with my coat pockets stuffed full, plodded to make up with her.

Anetė lived on the next street, on the opposite side of the kitchen-gardens, in a wooden two-storey building with two entrances. Each of my steps was slower than the last. I missed her like some looney lunatic (I knew such ones existed because my brother had told me), but I really begrudged the candies too.

I was sheepish to be the first to succumb. In their churned up yard – not a patch of clean snow – was a parked truck with four small trees in the corners of the bed. A few men I'd never seen before loitered by the entrance, smoking. Suddenly, Anetė walked

Vidas

out the door. She wore a funny grey nightdress, obviously too big for her. In March! She ignored the men, and me too. Like she didn't even see us. Neither of them looked her way; they just went on smoking and talking quietly as though nothing had happened. Annoyed, I stuck my tongue out at her. I had no idea where she was off to in that ugly nightdress of hers. But in a moment, she was gone. Well, I'll just leave her these damned candies for when she returns, I thought. I'll take them up the stairs and put them by her door. Then it will be goodbye forever, and I'll find another girl. We'll see what she says then!

Somewhat unsure, I climbed up the treacherous, hideously squeaky stairs on which spruce boughs had been placed on every step. If I'm nurturing my patience, what would be best, I wondered: to go through to the very end or to turn and run home as fast as my legs can carry me? I decided to keep at least one of the candies for myself; I chose the *Karakumai* and put it on the bend of the handrail to retrieve on my way back. At that moment, a strange woman passed by, headed downstairs. She scowled at me, as if I were some sort of culprit.

When I finally reached the second floor, the door of Anetė's home stood ajar. I heard quiet noises inside, sobbing and whispering. A spruce branch crunched under my foot. After stepping tentatively over the threshold, I crossed the hall and stopped in the living room doorway. The window here was covered with a black cloth, printed with dark green ornaments. Candles crackled as they burned and a mixture of smells floated around the room. Upset-looking people filled the benches along the walls. Some were neighbours I knew. On a dais in the middle of the room there was a small, brown coffin heaped with flowers. Two tin letters were stuck to the end of it. I didn't know who was lying there. All I could see from the doorway were the soles of the small shoes, the bluish knuckles of the clasped fingers, and the tip of an utterly unattractive nose. A woman in black approached me, her face red, her eyes puffy. She picked me up – I smelt vodka on her breath – and brought me closer to her daughter's coffin.

How is that possible, her lying here in a beautiful white dress with a little lace hat on her head? I thought. I've just seen her outside, in that stupid old grey nightdress.

Morkūnas

*****/the have-nots

On a feast day, Genovaitė M. was sitting in the churchyard where she was approached by a bearded man who politely offered to trade her prayer-book for his own. Taken aback just a little – was this some wicked ruse? – without much further consideration she handed the man her ancient, shabby book, with its greasy, dog-eared pages, and in return received a brand new one with firmly bound pages and a pleasant smelling leather cover. With this, the encounter was over.

In a fiction of the same event, old Genovaitė M. – she'd be given a different name of course – would probably believe it was God Himself who'd come out to His backyard to take a look around and decided to reward His humble daughter thus, to reward or maybe even test her. In fiction, she would probably miss her old prayer-book, its dear almost breathing pages, each caressed by her fingers so many times, each one bound up with one memory or another... And so on. But this is not fiction. Not art. In reality, the exchange didn't induce any particular thoughts in Genovaitė M., and didn't change anything in her life or alter her destiny in any way. The thought that God Himself could be right here, walking in the churchyard on the feast, never even occurred to the woman. God, in her opinion, had to be sitting somewhere aloft, untouched by earthly dust, where the sight and chatter of humanity couldn't reach Him.

Genovaitė M. put the book into her reticule, which had a shiny binding and a rusty buckle, and took out a bundle with some bread and hard-boiled eggs wrapped inside. What was it he said? *Life is as smooth as a shell?* There!

And yet later, back home, when her grandson inquired about the new prayer-book, Genovaitė M. had lied, saying she had bought it for herself...

Vidas

***/the rich

She was aware that she would not live long or like other people. She knew her looks. Nobody tried to hide the mirrors from her, nobody guarded her from catching a glimpse of her reflection in the water or on any other smooth surface. Her family wasn't that silly. Strangers, however, reacted in one of two ways. Some involuntarily averted their eyes, pretending not to have noticed. Others stared at her curiously, not even trying to hide their attempts to guess... congenital deformity? Terrible accident? Divine retribution? The majority of votes went ignorantly to the latter. And people, as you know, tend to transpose their assumptions into facts.

I saw her for the first time from the bus as it pulled up at the stop next to where she lived. The iron post to which was attached a battered, scratched tin that would rattle on windy days and nights. It used to hold a timetable, which had now faded to illegibility. I caught only a glimpse of her in the slushy yard – it was almost always boggy, in rainy summers, in sleety springs, in warm winters – only a short glimpse of her face, a false face, I thought for a moment; actually, the very moment felt false, and a foreboding overcame me, a sense that I had peeked uninvited at something, some forbidden reality, and now a punishment of some sort hung over me. Only later would I learn that the face was quite real.

She stroked a hairy dog frolicking in the yard and went to a yellowing, rugged grassland beyond the village. She never visited the holiday resort just nineteen kilometres away, bustling with life in summers and quietening only with autumn well underway. What it was like, and what the sea was like, she didn't know. The bushy grasslands were her resort. The sun, though somewhat dimmed by fluffy clouds, was hot enough to bring drops of sweat to her gnarled forehead. As usual, she turned this way and that until she felt the direction of a mild wind, then exposed her flat bosom to it, reclined her heavy head, and closed her eyes. The lazy easterly quickly dried the cool drops, so only the biggest rolled down the large knob of her face, crossed the hollow of the empty eye-socket and, moving sideways, the big, flat nose devoid of nostrils; where it turned around and hung for a moment over the second, smaller knob, the little nose with one nostril, leaned up against it. Then again it rolled on, along her twisted, chapped and purulent lip, down the triple flaps of her chin – the biggest of the three receding as if lopped off with an axe, before ending its journey in a tuft of hair.

    The dog sauntered over the grassland and sat down by her feet. The pain had subsided for now. The heaviness on her heart had thawed.

Vidas

***/the early

ᶜThe train was due in another four hours, so it was boredom rather than curiosity that drove Stasys R. to make the round of every nook of the station and read the timetable three times.

The platform's tarmac, creased as it was, still held in front of the station; but, further on, it was already crumbling on both sides of the rails and grass sprouted sunward in the fissures. Around the red-brick water tower with a boarded-up door, chickens pecked the dirt, and a fat cat squinted from on top of the post of a wooden fence.

Somehow Stasys R. had not forgotten the stack of crossties at the end of the platform – the ties had already been cluttered there when he last left this station ten years ago. Blackened now, the lower ones overgrown and glued to the ground, they still smelled pleasantly of oil, creosote, and motion.

After four hours of solid boredom, with the time to board the train approaching, he sat down on a worn, hard, bench and remained sitting there.

He realised with a start that rather than boarding the train, he'd instead begun to walk home, a journey of at least seventy kilometres on foot. He walked along a dusty track. It passed through a green meadow overgrown with bushes. Both grass and bushes seemed completely still. Every so often, Stasys R. turned back, and each time felt a sudden bout of unease. Instead of receding, the forest behind him seemed to draw closer. He noticed something white among the willows on his left and without a second thought headed towards it, as though summoned. A large square of canvas was laid over the tall grass by the bushes, on which was printed a full-length portrait of Stasys R.'s mother early in her life, like an old sepia photograph. My mother was so gorgeous back then, he realised. A sudden breeze rippled the canvas, causing Stasys R. to imagine his mother's face distorting, her body falling into a fit of convulsions. Disgusted, he turned away and again caught sight of something white, this time in the branches of a nearby osier. He waded over and saw a shroud draped, carrying a full-length portrait of his little brother who had died as a young child. He was smiling in his grey shirt and his strapped shorts. The shroud was spread and crumpled unevenly such that the child's smile looked like a horrendous grimace and his body appeared broken. The greenery around was thinning, more and more so; white shrouds with portraits like patches of dirty snow were everywhere covering the grass, the shrubs, the branches of trees. Stasys R. slopped among them, as though trying to walk through snowdrifts, ignoring the track, looking intently for something, stepping on the printed bodies of people long dead and those not so long gone, of family members, relatives, friends, and others unremembered, but somehow apparently connected to him in one way or another. Rushes of wind heaved and flapped the sheets and it seemed as though the dead were trying to rise with every last ounce of their strength, eager to escape a tight grip. In vain. Finally he found it – he'd arrived at the thing he'd been looking for. The square of canvas, spread out on the flat stretch of ground, pure white, freshly starched. No print on it at all.

Vidas

***/the have-nots

For thirty years, Elvyra S. led the morning exercises in the factory which made parts for wind instruments. Throughout this time, she had applied her own unique method to these exercises, one she hoped would radically revolutionise the fitness world, though every attempt to publish a handbook written years ago had failed.

Every morning before eight, the manufacturers rallied in the assembly hall of the factory for fifteen minutes before work to play at being deer. The factory workers she trained did not waggle or stretch, they did not squat or jump. Such primitive expressions would not suit Elvyra S.'s artistic ambitions, they would injure her creative dignity. Instead they trundled along the slippery parquet, wiggling their buttocks, their crossed hands raised above their heads, fingers outstretched.

Even on her very first day on the job, however, Elvyra S. realised that she would not find any worthy apprentices in this crowd. She feared that none could be trained to her level. Sadly, her fears were confirmed. Over a span of three decades, cadres came and went but in all that abundance only a few workers showed the slightest aptitude. They may be able to carve perfect reeds for French horns, but their deer were lousy. It seemed like the only people who came to work in the factory were hopeless lubbers, bumpkins with no sense of spirituality. Elvyra S. was particularly offended by their apparent indifference. Patiently, however, she persevered in trying to make them understand the Stanislavskian Task, the throughline of action, but the slouches didn't even care.

Years passed, the workers changed, but not the attitude, the determination to somehow fail to learn anything from these fifteen minutes and then steal a moment for a smoke before turning to the mouthpieces, valves, and pipes. The more zealously Elvyra S. plumbed the depths of the psychology, physiology, behavioural patterns, and anatomy of deer, eager to pass on her knowledge to the assembled staff, the more openly and defiantly the manufacturers ignored her efforts. She was sure that in order to authentically render the movements of this elegant animal, one must know the forest from which it hails, its age, what it has nibbled recently, the number of rutting seasons it went through, the diseases it succumbed to, and so on. But their crooked grins, their faces full of boredom, their clumsy flumping made Elvyra S. completely frustrated. She realised, painfully, that she had sacrificed the best years of her life to too brilliant an idea for these God-forsaken oafs to grasp. If only she hadn't left the promising enterprise making mesh nets for tennis rackets. Everyone had tried to persuade her to stay. Ah...

A human aspect was important to the enterprise of making parts for wind instruments. Those who broke records for productivity were granted a place in the Gallery of Honour; the retiring veterans were graced with The Copper Tonality Prize statuettes; the deceased members of the staff – especially the ones who happened to expire at the premises – were solemnly mourned.

After changing into her exercise attire, Elvyra S. used the service entrance to reach the small stage of the assembly hall, and there she stopped, petrified. Two huge digits carved neatly out of plywood hung on the wall above the stage: 3 and 0. Meticulously plastered with colourful shards from broken Christmas decorations, the three and the zero glistened prettily, touched by the rays of sunlight seeping in through neglected windows. For the first time in the three decades that Elvyra S.'s had worked here, the whole staff had gathered to exercise, from the watchwoman to the director. Each person was clad in a brand new grey robe and on each of their heads was a pair of rubber foam antlers made specifically for the occasion. Instructed in advance by the factory's spokeswoman, the deer bellowed in unison and, holding onto their wavering, shaky antlers, eagerly started to exercise.

Tears welled in Elvyra S.'s eyes.

Bibliography & Bibliographical Notes

Death
From *Report from an Egg* (Lithuanian Writers' Union Publishing House, 2012)

This short story won the Second Prize of the *Dirva*, the American Lithuanian Weekly, the Antanas Vienuolis-Žukauskas Museum National Short Story Contest award and Antanas Vaičiulaitis award.

It also has been translated into Georgian and Ukrainian.

Everyone's Neighbour
From *Report from an Egg*, which was shortlisted for the Most Creative Book Award in 2012.

Social Science For Pheasants
From *Report from an Egg* (Lithuanian Writers' Union Publishing House, 2012)

Pakeleivingų Stotys
From *Pakeleivingų stotys* (*Wayfarers Stations*, Odilė, 2019) which won the 'Most Creative Book' award in 2019.

***/encaustic
This story was translated into Latvian and English for the International Riga Prose Festival.

***/the wealthy
This story was translated into Polish.

***/the early
This story was translated into English, published in Vilnius Review online journal.

***/the have-nots
This story was translated into English, published in Vilnius Review online journal.

KŪNAI, meaning 'bodies', is a series of five chapbooks showcasing writing never-before-seen in English from a diverse selection of the finest contemporary writers and translators working in Lithuanian today.

It is the result of Strangers Press' latest exciting collaboration with an international group of authors, translators, publishers, designers and editors, all made possible by generous funding from The Lithuanian Culture Institute.

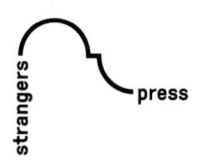

Lithuanian Culture Institute

strangers press

University of East Anglia

NORWICH
UNIVERSITY
OF THE ARTS